Lisa: Book Four

HAVE I FOUND
A GOLD MINE?

PRISCILLA GALLOWAY

**Look for the other Lisa stories
in Our Canadian Girl**

LISA: BOOK FOUR

HAVE I FOUND A GOLD MINE?

PRISCILLA GALLOWAY

PENGUIN
CANADA

JP Gallo
28 11 07
Copy 2
910

PENGUIN CANADA

Published by the Penguin Group

Penguin Group (Canada), 90 Eglinton Avenue East, Suite 700, Toronto, Ontario, Canada
M4P 2Y3 (a division of Pearson Canada Inc.)

Penguin Group (USA) Inc., 375 Hudson Street, New York, New York 10014, U.S.A.
Penguin Books Ltd, 80 Strand, London WC2R 0RL, England
Penguin Ireland, 25 St Stephen's Green, Dublin 2, Ireland (a division of Penguin Books Ltd)
Penguin Group (Australia), 250 Camberwell Road, Camberwell, Victoria 3124, Australia
(a division of Pearson Australia Group Pty Ltd)
Penguin Books India Pvt Ltd, 11 Community Centre, Panchsheel Park, New Delhi – 110 017, India
Penguin Group (NZ), 67 Apollo Drive, Rosedale, North Shore 0632, New Zealand
(a division of Pearson New Zealand Ltd)
Penguin Books (South Africa) (Pty) Ltd, 24 Sturdee Avenue, Rosebank, Johannesburg 2196,
South Africa

Penguin Books Ltd, Registered Offices: 80 Strand, London WC2R 0RL, England

First published 2007

1 2 3 4 5 6 7 8 9 10   (WEB)

Copyright © Priscilla Galloway, 2007
Illustrations copyright © Don Kilby, 2007
Design: Matthews Communications Design Inc.
Map copyright © Sharon Matthews

Manufactured in Canada.

Library and Archives Canada Cataloguing in Publication data available upon request.

ISBN-13: 978-0-14-305446-7
ISBN-10: 0-14-305446-5

Visit the Penguin Group (Canada) website at **www.penguin.ca**

Special and corporate bulk purchase rates available; please see
www.penguin.ca/corporatesales or call 1-800-810-3104, ext. 477 or 474

For my son Glenn

with love

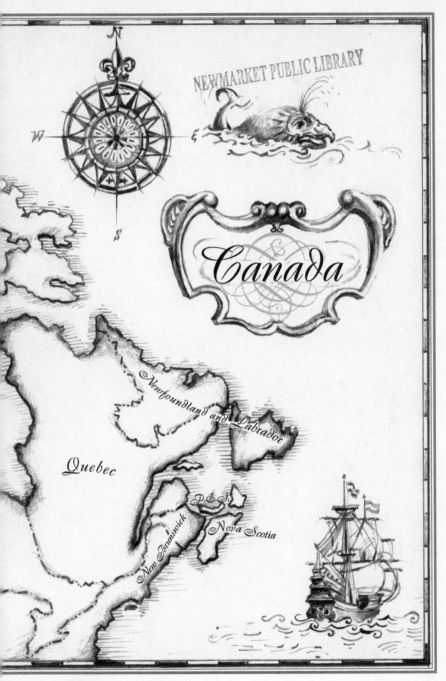

Canada

N
W E
S

Newfoundland and Labrador

Quebec

P.E.I.

Nova Scotia

New Brunswick

 Marks the location of the story

FINDING GOLD ON YOUR PROPERTY DOESN'T MEAN YOU OWN A MINE

RESEARCHING AND WRITING the four books of the Lisa series has been a rich and happy experience for me, taking me back into my own family history and my early married life in mining towns.

When my husband, Bev Galloway, graduated in 1950, he was hired as mine geologist at Quesabe Gold Mine in Northern Quebec. We moved to Rouyn-Noranda, and Bev began his underground career.

Underground mining is dirty, cold, and dangerous. It is also incredibly dark. This I myself experienced when Bev had been at Quesabe for almost a year and the mine manager, his assistant, and Bev took me down to the 180-metre level. We walked away from the rickety cage until we had turned a corner, and then one by one we turned off the lamps in the hard hats we all wore.

Blackness, no glimmer of light anywhere. Waiting for our eyes to adjust made no difference at all. I am not usually claustrophobic, but the blackness pressed in on me and I have never forgotten it.

Through Bev's mining and exploration jobs, I learned the economics of mining. When Lisa finds a seam of gold, don't they have a mine?

Maybe; maybe not. Ore is rock with mineral content that can be extracted at a profit. There may be gold in the rock, but if you can't get it out and sell it for more than it costs to extract it, then it's rock, not ore, and you don't have a mine.

The same rock may not be ore this year, but may be next. How can this be?

If the price of gold goes up, then many formerly worthless deposits may become mines. If somebody finds a cheaper way to get the rock out of the ground or to extract the mineral from it, the rock becomes ore. New mines spring up and old ones are pumped out and put back into production. Quesabe was a small mine and the price of gold in 1950 was low. The mine closed shortly before our second Christmas in the north. Later, my husband worked in the Cobalt area, the site of Canada's richest silver discoveries early in the twentieth century. A few silver mines were still operating then, fifty years after the boom, though almost all are closed now.

Wellington Delaney Moses, one of a small group of black immigrants, came to the Cariboo from San Francisco by way of Victoria. Known as the Black Barber of Barkerville, he really did help police to identify and catch a murderer. His hair tonic was famous, and the words I have quoted actually appeared on his label. My grandfather's shaving mug is the model for Archie McNaughton's.

Augustus Schubert did lose a lawsuit over a claim and had to pull his stakes, though it happened later than the time of my story. The two Schubert daughters, Mary Jane and Rose, both attended St. Ann's Academy, the convent school run by the Sisters of St. Ann in New Westminster. The Boarders' Accounts Ledger for September 1870 records their fees as $32.50 per month. All the girls at St. Ann's slept on single beds in a big dormitory. The regime was spartan. The girls had a hot bath once a week; if anyone wanted to bathe more often, she had to use cold water.

The Cariboo was Canada's first major gold rush. Compared with the California gold rush, ten years earlier in the United States, and with the Klondike rush, thirty-five years later, it was not huge. Few men made fortunes; fewer still kept them. Nobody ever found the fabled "motherlode," that vast seam of gold from which many prospectors believed that the nuggets in the rivers had come. There was no motherlode in the Cariboo.

The gold was there, but it was dispersed and therefore difficult and expensive to recover. Individual miners were soon bought out by big companies with enough money to bring a mine into production, but that came later than Lisa's story.

Lisa's adventures began in Book 1 with an epic journey overland from present-day Winnipeg to Kamloops in British Columbia's interior. They continued in Book 2 with another hazardous trip to the mining country, where Lisa almost immediately found a rich gold nugget. In Book 3, Lisa discovered that the nugget might not belong to her, even though she had found it. Finding gold brings problems as well as rewards.

Lisa, Book 4, concludes this series. Lisa and her partners may or may not be among the lucky few who have found a mine. Lisa's papa, Augustus Schubert, arrived in Cameronton early in the fall of 1863, soon after Lisa found her second nugget. On the way, Papa bought a claim from another man from Fort Garry. Soon, however, his rights were challenged in court. Papa had worked long days as a carpenter and builder in Kamloops and Lillooet. Ma had scrimped and saved. Would they be cheated out of everything? How could Lisa help them?

Fever swept through the Cariboo mining towns in the winter of 1862. The towns pooled resources to build a small hospital in the fall of 1863. Churches were gradually built, though they were always hugely outnumbered by the saloons. Merchants, lawyers, and tradesmen arrived and opened their doors. Educated folk offered to teach illiterate miners how to read and write. A lending library, Literary Society, Drama Society, and other organizations further enhanced the cultural and social life of the towns.

Did Lisa want to be a miner the same way a six-year-old boy might want to be a fireman? Or would her ambition be lasting? As a single young woman, how could she keep from being cheated herself? How could she help her family?

CHAPTER N°. 1

August 31, 1863, Cameronton, the Cariboo

I had been in the Cariboo only two months, and already I had found gold, twice! I, Lisa Schubert, age eleven and a half!

The first time happened the day after I came to town. It was only one nugget, and I found it by smashing up a rock that my partners had thrown away, only not really, and for a while I never thought I'd get to keep it, so maybe that didn't count.

The second time, though, happened just the day before this. I was a partner now, along with

Archie and Mrs. McNaughton, James Wattie, Davie Ross, and Adam Bailey.

For more than a month, I searched for a place where my mortal enemy Samuel Stokes had been digging on his own. I bought Samuel's claim; that's how I got to be a partner.

Then I found it, only it was a tunnel, an adit. The entrance was a cleft in the rocky hillside hidden by brambles. I'd never have found it if I hadn't been looking. Poor Samuel Stokes. If he were not such a nasty man, I could almost feel sorry for him. But I didn't. He had lied to and cheated everybody. It looked as if he had found a few nuggets of gold in the adit, but only a few. He had left town three weeks earlier. By now, surely, he was far away. He could not go too far for me.

A rock slide had almost blocked the tunnel. I had climbed over the rocks, and my hands still stung where Mr. Wattie and Archie whipped me because I didn't go and get them first. I hate it when grown-ups punish me and then tell me it's for my own good, but I did do a stupid thing, so I guess they were right—that time, anyway. If more rocks had fallen or if my lantern had run out of oil, I might never have got out alive.

But I found four nuggets and—much more important—a seam of gold. A seam, even a skinny one, can run for a long way. We might have a rich mine, and I found it.

We were all as excited as anybody could possibly be last evening. Supper was long over and the table cleared when Mrs. Mac stood up. "This is the wrong evening for Lisa and me to read you the latest installment of Mr. Dickens's new novel," she said. With a rustle of skirts, she glided gracefully toward her elegant little organ. Two men had struggled to carry it over the muddy trail after we came to the end of the wagon road. One saloon in town boasted an organ, but ours was the only one in somebody's house.

"Gather round, everybody, and let's sing," she said. We gathered, and sang with a will— "Alouette," "Greensleeves," "The Vicar of Bray,"

"Men of Harlech," song after cheery song. I knew all the verses of most of them. If I forgot a line, Archie's light tenor or James Wattie's powerful bass quickly provided the cue.

How could I ever get to sleep after that? I did, though, and the sun was well up in the sky when the smell of bacon and of coffee woke me, and it was the first day of September, and I knew it would be a perfect day.

CHAPTER N.º 2

Mrs. Mac still sat at the table when I stumbled down the stairs, wiping sleep from my eyes. Usually I made breakfast, or at least started the fire.

"Mrs. Mac," I gulped. "You must think I'm a lazybones. I'm really sorry. What a day to over-sleep."

"This one time, it's no matter, Lisa," said Mrs. Mac gently. "You were late to bed. Naturally, you are not early to rise. But I was ready to wake you. We don't want to be late at the hospital building."

Red flooded my face. "How could I forget?" I said. Only two weeks earlier, Judge Begbie and Gold Commissioner O'Reilly had put spades in the ground to begin the foundation for our new hospital. Today was building day—like a barn raising back east, only we weren't putting up a barn for a neighbour; we were building a hospital for everybody on Williams Creek, in all the mining towns—prospectors, too, when they were hurt. "If you are ready, Ma'am," I added, "I won't wait for breakfast. There will be plenty to eat at Marysville."

"The men left an hour ago," Mrs. Mac told me, "but we do not need to rush. There's toast and an egg for you. I've packed our basket, not forgetting enamel plates and mugs, so eat up, Lisa, and then we'll go."

I smiled. Mrs. Mac had never been to a barn raising. I had told her what we should do, and I had baked extra bread and cooked up a big crock of beans and salt pork, sweetened with molasses. Our basket would be heavy, but the two of us could carry it well enough.

My toast and egg vanished, and I saucered my tea and gulped it. Mrs. Mac raised her eyebrows but said nothing. Drinking from the saucer used to be accepted in the best circles, but these days it is not something a lady should do. However, even Mrs. Mac will let some things pass, though not often, and I was thankful she said no word of reproach.

Mr. James Wattie—our own Mr. Wattie—was chairman of the Hospital Board, and in charge of the building. The foundation was ready. "If enough miners join in, we'll have the walls up and the roof on in one day," Mr. Wattie had said.

Of course we all wanted to go. Archie and Mr. Wattie had agreed we need not leave anybody on guard, though Davie Ross had promised to check our diggings on his way home.

Even with the heavy basket between us, Mrs. Mac and I walked quickly. Marysville was west of Cameronton, and not far, though it was not growing like Barkerville, which got nearer to Cameronton with every new house. If we hadn't known the way, we'd have found it fast enough with all the noise—axes crashing, saws whining, mallets thudding, men yelling to be heard.

As we entered the yard, women were unpacking their baskets, loading food onto makeshift trestle tables under the trees. A couple of men staggered as they carried a huge leather bucket full of water, dangling from a wooden yoke that lay across their shoulders. While we watched, they bent their knees until the bucket rested on the ground. Some of the workers downed tools and gathered, panikins in hand, to ladle out water. They drank great gulps, then poured the rest over their hot faces or over the hair that seemed to be plastered to their heads already, perhaps with sweat.

Archie waved to us from the nearest wall before he signalled his men to lift the next squared log into place. Other men, their hands full of wet grey clay, slapped the mortar into every chink. As the mortar dried, it would shrink, and more big cracks would appear. Men would

Archie waved to us from the nearest wall before he signalled his men to lift the next squared log into place.

chink new cracks for years before the logs were completely dry. This winter, wind would blow through many an opening. None could be too small for wind and snow to find their way. Next winter would be better, and the winter after better still.

I wandered among the loaded tables, lifting linen covers to peek at plates of cheese, bread, and butter; and at pans or crocks of baked beans— some dark with sweet molasses, like mine, some light-coloured, with onions and carrots poking through. There was cold roast; and there was head cheese, a jelly with the meat from a pig's head and trotters cut up and mixed in. Just the smell made me hungry for it.

Head cheese was one of Ma's specialties. Mrs. Mac says seeing and smelling a pig's head was enough for her and she'd have to be pretty hungry before she boiled it and made meat jelly, though she had liked head cheese before she knew how it was made. At that moment, I missed Ma so hard my stomach hurt; then I moved on.

There was a tall bowl that looked like whipped cream. I slipped in my finger and licked it. Trifle! Yum-m-m-m-m-m. Apple pies, a cherry pie, lumpy squares, and bars of cookies. I was ready for dinner any time.

Right at noon, Mr. Wattie blew his whistle and called the crew to eat. The new preacher, Reverend John Evans from Wales, said the blessing, a long one, calling on God to give the miners strength on this day and to bless the new hospital and the doctors and nurses, and the patients too, that those who recovered should be thankful and that those who died should gladly accept God's will.

I would not want Reverend Evans to visit me if I was sick, or to visit anybody else in my family. I would fight to stay alive. Maybe it would be God's will for me to do that, though. When I try to make sense of some things, my head aches.

At last Reverend Evans finished talking to God. Mr. Wattie thanked the men for working and the ladies for the food. He asked the men to sign a petition asking the government in Victoria for money for medicine and bandages and other things the hospital would need, but he said that our hospital would open anyhow before the end of October and that he had hired Dr. Walter Shaw Black as surgeon. Dr. Black was deeply tanned, with a neat pointed beard the same colour as his name. He had trained in London and had come to the Cariboo all the way from the gold rushes in Australia. The doctor said he looked forward to serving in our hospital, bowed, and sat down again. Everybody cheered, partly I think because he did not make a long speech.

The men helped themselves first. It had been the same in Fort Garry: the ladies had to wait. We didn't wait long, though, because there were no chairs at the tables. The men took their loaded plates and sat, some on stumps or logs, others on their coats or on rugs the ladies had brought. They all had their kits, including a plate and mug, knife, fork, and spoon.

I had my plate ready, not far from the head cheese. It was painful to see how many men took big slices of it. Would there be any for me? When there were only two pieces left, Mrs. Bowron from the Wake Up, Jake Restaurant came along with a second bowl as big as the first. Now *that* was worth being thankful for, and I was, to God and to Mrs. Bowron as well.

I cut off one mouthful with my fork and ate it right away. It was almost like being home with Ma and Papa and Gus, Mary Jane, Jamie, and baby Rose. I helped myself to bread and butter and two kinds of pickles, some side pork and beans, and a piece of apple pie, in case there was none left when I was ready for it. Mrs. Mac had spread her brown rug in the sun; even at midday, the air was cool. All us partners sat near each other: Mr. Wattie, Archie and Mrs. Mac, Davie Ross, and Adam Bailey—and me.

"I see four walls," said Mrs. Mac. "Well done, gentlemen." She raised her mug of tea in a toast and sipped it politely.

"The walls are rising," Mr. Wattie agreed. "Not high enough yet, but we'll get there."

"Are we running low on timbers?" That was Adam's voice. He was a timid man, who seldom said anything at all, so his question was a surprise.

"You think so?" asked Mr. Wattie.

Adam nodded.

"I'll put a party to squaring more timbers as soon as we've finished our dinner. Thank you, Adam. Have you made any estimate of lumber needed for the inside walls?"

Of course I wanted to know what rooms there would be.

"Three," answered Archie. "One ward, a doctor's office, and a kitchen."

"What accommodation is there for female patients?" asked Mrs. Mac at once.

"None, to start with," Mr. Wattie replied bluntly. "We hope a woman can be cared for at home. If she must be in the hospital for a day or two, we will put up a screen beside her bed. Females may be the weaker sex, Ma'am, but they don't have machinery or rocks falling on them like the mining men, nor do they come in with toes or fingers frozen, like prospectors do, often enough, in the winter."

"I understand," said Mrs. Mac quietly, but I could see she was not happy about it. Nor was I. I'd been burned often enough at the stove, or scalded over the laundry, and so had Ma, though we were both careful. A woman in Kamloops had cut off her finger with an axe while chopping wood. Sophia Cameron had died of fever in the Cariboo.

I stood up. "Would anybody like a piece of pie?" I asked brightly. "I'd be pleased to bring it—if there is any left."

The men held out their plates. "I'd best come with you, Lisa," said Mrs. Mac.

We walked through a buzz of chatter toward the tables. Everybody works so hard that we don't often take time to get together; this day was special. Two billowing hooped skirts suddenly blocked our way. Hurdy-gurdies! Here were my friends Fraulein Lili and Fraulein Greta, who danced every night with the miners at one of the saloons. Mrs. Mac had been sure they were no fit company for me, but after I had saved Fraulein Greta from marrying Samuel Stokes, she had changed her mind. Fraulein Greta hugged me, forcing her hoops up behind her.

"How are you both?" asked Mrs. Mac warmly. She always said that the true mark of a lady was that no one should be made to feel uncomfortable because of her station in life. My hurdy-gurdy friends had been made very uncomfortable indeed; now Mrs. Mac was extra careful. Besides, she liked them both, now that she knew them.

Fraulein Lili spoke good English, since she had come from Germany by way of California; she did most of the talking, though Fraulein Greta understood almost everything.

"You know I plan to go back to California this winter," Lili said. "But I'll wait until Greta's lawsuits are settled." Greta was suing several companies and individuals, trying to recover the money that Samuel Stokes had cheated her out of. He had borrowed money from anybody who would lend it, as soon as there had been a public announcement that he and Greta would soon be married. Samuel Stokes had no money, but Greta had saved quite a lot.

One or two people had settled when there had been no marriage after all; Greta would not have to pay back what Samuel had borrowed from them. Some of Samuel's bad dealings were more complicated, however; two lawsuits were pending, with perhaps a third to come. "In court, I translate what Greta says," said Lili. "That way, maybe she won't be cheated any more."

"I dance every night," said Greta. "Pay lawyer."

"You look tired," I said. "Are you working too hard?"

"Silly, I work same as always." Greta's chin came up. She had been very lively, but all of a sudden she turned pale.

Lili looked at her anxiously. "We were ready to start for home," she said, "but then we saw both of you, and of course we had to say hello. Now we must go. Come see us soon, yes?"

"I'd like you to come to tea with us," said Mrs. Mac at once. "Would Thursday afternoon suit?"

We agreed on a time, and the two women began their walk. It was perhaps three miles—no great distance—but Fraulein Greta's steps dragged a little, even at the start.

"She does not look well," said Mrs. Mac. "Perhaps we can persuade her not to dance every night."

The men ate their pie quickly and gathered their tools. "Everybody has a job except me," I complained. "Can I come and help? Please, Mr. Wattie?"

"Come along," he said. "I'll find a job for you."

So I chinked the walls, rubbing handfuls of wet clay into the spaces between the timbers, and got a nasty sliver in my hand, which Dr. Walter Shaw Black removed with a needle and a pair of tweezers, not as gently as Ma would have done.

CHAPTER N° 3

There was a hard frost that night, and a snowstorm—the first of the season—the next day. For three days, the wind howled and the wet flakes fell, drifting against the door, piling up on the window ledges. We had to keep our lantern going most of the day.

Mrs. Mac worried. "I'm not ready for winter," she said.

"This snow will melt." Archie replied. "Tell me what supplies you still need, my love. I'll ask James to lend me his pony cart to fetch them home."

Archie was right. The skies cleared. The sun shone, though weakly, and the snow melted into muddy rivulets that filled the ruts in the road. And—Papa arrived. He knocked on the door late in the afternoon. I was late with my baking that day, as I'd been inside the adit all morning, digging in the clay floor. There were no more gold nuggets, though. Not yet.

"Papa!" I flung myself into his arms and he held me tight.

For a while we both kept talking at the same time, interrupting each other. "When did you leave, Papa? How's Ma? How's the baby? Your beard is really long." I could make personal remarks any time to Papa!

"How tall you are, Lisa! Quite the lady." I was wearing my old gingham dress and my apron was full of flour and smudged with soot from the stove. I had been almost ready to change before Archie came home. Papa's eyes were weaker than they had been if he really thought I looked like a lady. I didn't mind, though. Oh, how I loved him!

How had I stood it, being without my family for so long?

Papa had just arrived in Cameronton. He had to stay at James Seller's roadhouse at Beaver Lake because of the storm. "Lucky thing for me, that storm," he said. "Tell you more about it later." Papa grinned. He polished his spectacles so hard I thought he'd make a hole in his handkerchief.

"Is there a boarding house nearby?" Papa asked, looking at Mrs. Mac. "Or should I stay at a hotel?"

"Augustus, I wish I could invite you to stay here." Mrs. Mac sighed. "All we could offer would be a straw mattress on the floor by the fire. Do take your meals with us, though. Lisa is a good plain cook, and I lend a hand myself."

"Oh yes, Papa, you must come," I burst in.

Archie opened the door in time to add his persuasions, and I jumped up to take my bread and the stew out of the oven. After supper, Archie and Papa went out to the back of the house. They decided Papa would pitch his tent there until the winter froze him out. "I may look for a cabin here," said Papa. "Ma likely won't move until spring. Maybe she will, though, if I have a house for the family. I'm going to stay, for sure." He kept grinning fit to split his face.

"You look like the cat that swallowed the canary," I said. That's what Ma would have told him, if she had been here. "Papa, what is going on?"

"Do tell us," said Mrs. Mac.

"I smell a story," Archie chimed in.

We moved our chairs close to the fire, and Archie put on another log.

"My luck has changed," Papa began. "Every traveller hunkered down somewhere to wait out the storm. I don't know if they all played poker, but that's what they did at Seller's, everybody but me. Not that I take against the game, but I have no luck at the gaming table, and I know it."

Archie nodded. "Your face tells too much, Augustus. I have warned you, haven't I?"

Papa nodded. "You have, and Ma as well," he said. "Even if I had taken a hand or two, though, I'd have quit when the stakes went up. A pity

Eric Firman didn't know himself a little better."
He looked at each of us in turn, as if daring
anybody to interrupt. We stayed silent. "You'll
be wondering who Eric Firman is," he added.
Papa is too good at suspense.

"Papa, hurry up," I begged. "Tell us now!"

"Right," said Papa. "It turned into a wicked
game, and Eric Firman played with a dead man's
money as well as his own. He lost every cent, plus
fifty dollars he didn't have, and got drunk into
the bargain. What a fool! His father farmed
outside Fort Garry, a decent man; he used to buy
his whiskey from me.

"The dead man was Firman's partner, killed in
a rock slide a couple of weeks ago. He was on his
way east to tell the wife she was a widow now,
and not a rich one; her assets were a half-share in
a mining claim plus a little cash money. Eric had
hoped to buy her half-share. Now he could not
do that. Worse, he had no way of raising the extra
fifty dollars. He would have to sell the claim in
order to settle his debt.

"He hoped I would help him," Papa went on. "'You hope I'll help you cheat a widow woman?'" Papa's eyebrows went up, as if Mr. Firman were still in front of him. "The young man did turn red, and well he might."

We all made little noises of disapproval.

"He said the widow could have every cent he got for the claim," Papa told us. "Except, of course, for the fifty dollars and travel expenses to Fort Garry. But he had to sell the claim to somebody right away. Would I—Augustus Schubert—buy it?

"I said I'd sleep on it," Papa continued, "but then Eric began talking to everybody in the place. Most of them had been in the Cariboo. They had spent all their money and were going home. They were a bitter lot. But two or three were like me, on their way. Some people do find gold, we all know that. One man had his pencil out, figuring. This was *my* chance for a bargain, and I didn't want to lose it.

"I made him an offer and we settled the deal that night."

"So you got it cheap," said Archie. "But is it any good, this claim? Has anybody spent money on it, or found anything?"

"I've found gold—again," I said. "Our claims are good, aren't they, Archie?"

Papa's eyes swivelled to me, then back to Archie.

"Maybe," said Archie. "Or maybe not. We'll know better come spring. Meanwhile, we are not speaking of it. I understand why you've told your Papa, Lisa, but there it must stop." Archie could be just as stern as Mr. Wattie sometimes. I said I was sorry, and that I wouldn't forget again. "I'll explain tomorrow," Archie told Papa. "Go on with your story, Augustus, if you please."

"There are three claims on one side of my land," said Papa, "and two on the other. They belong to the Last Chance Company. That company is sinking a shaft. Firman is certain the miners have found gold; he believes there is a seam that leads toward my property. It all seemed like a sure thing at the time, but it does not seem nearly as likely now."

"Most of us believe something we truly want to believe," said Mrs. Mac quietly, "sometimes, at least. However it turns out, Augustus, you did a kind deed for a widow."

"I didn't really," said Papa. "Young Firman may never give a penny to the widow. If he's right about the Last Chance property, I'll have cheated her, buying too cheap."

"You cannot know, one way or the other," said Mrs. Mac firmly. "It's just as likely you've cheated yourself."

"*More* likely," said Archie. "Most claims don't pan out." He grinned, and Mrs. Mac and I made faces at his bad pun. "Have you seen your property, Augustus?"

"Not yet," said Papa. "I thought Lisa might come with me tomorrow, if you can spare her. And yourself and Mrs. McNaughton too, I hope."

"Lisa, it's easy to guess what you want to do." Mrs. Mac's eyes smiled at me. "Go, by all means."

She turned to Papa. "Augustus, you must excuse me this time. I am taking tea in the afternoon with three or four other ladies. We wish to offer our services as helpers at the new hospital, and I must make a list of what our services might be."

Mrs. Mac had already joined the Literary Society, and she planned to start a drama and recitation league. Now she would find helpers for the hospital as well. I had yawned my way through two meetings of the Literary Society without wanting to read a single book. *Uncle Tom's Cabin*, by Mrs. Stowe, was next, and Mrs. Mac was writing a paper on it to read at the meeting. She had told me I'd like that book, but so far I had not borrowed it. Plays and poetry might be more interesting.

"I must also make my excuses," said Archie. "I'd best work on our property. You and Lisa will have a fine day together. You should register your change in ownership soon, though, and I will gladly come with you to Richfield. If I can introduce you to the gold commissioner, so much the better. If not, at least you'll meet the clerk. Day after tomorrow, will it suit you?"

Papa agreed.

CHAPTER N°. 4

I didn't sleep in the next day, but Papa was already building up the fire when I came downstairs. The sky was filled with rosy light, and, as I watched, the sun's rim glowed like gold above the horizon.

I fried bacon and browned slices of bread in the bacon grease for breakfast, and set the kettle to boil for coffee. We ate happily and I packed the rest for our lunch. Soon we were tramping along the muddy road.

My claim and the rest of ours were near Cariboo Cameron's mine, where seventy men still worked night and day digging out ore. Cariboo used a crusher to separate the gold from the plain rock. If the seam I found was big enough and went far enough, my partners and I could be as rich as Cariboo.

Papa's claim was in the other direction. I had explored this road, but had never walked this far along it.

"How will you know when we get there?" I asked.

"We'll see the Last Chance shaft," said Papa. "Then we'll look for my numbers." He was polishing his glasses while we walked, the way he always did when he was worried or excited.

I laughed. "I hope you find lots of gold," I told him.

The land near *our* claims was criss-crossed with flumes—wide wooden troughs that carried water for sluicing the gold out of the crushed ore. Along this road, there were no flumes, no machinery, no people. I pulled up a small yellow flower to add to my botanical collection. At last,

I saw a solitary digging not far away, one single shaft. The sky was that amazing deep blue of September, when the sun still has some warmth at midday, though the nights now were cold and would soon be colder. "I hope you can do some work on your claim before winter," I said.

"Me too," Papa agreed. "Lisa, what's the number on this stake? Maybe this marks my corner." He put his glasses back on his nose and took a paper from his pocket.

I read out the numbers while Papa checked them. He was right. I tied a piece of red cotton to the top of the wooden stake. Then Papa and I began searching for the other three markers. "I'm sure this is a lucky claim," I said.

We were still excited when a burly man strode up to Papa. "I'm Bert Rush, Clerk," he announced. "Do I address Mr. Augustus Schubert?"

"I am Mr. Schubert," Papa replied with dignity. "Have you business with me, sir?"

"I have, sir," was the rude response. "I'm here to say you have no right or title to this ground.

I am here, sir, to order you to pull up your stakes and leave this property. You are trespassing, sir, and I'm here to warn you off."

Papa turned a bewildered face, first to the man in front of him, then to me. "I don't understand," he said. "I bought this property. I can show you my bill of sale, signed and witnessed."

The man in front of him shrugged heavy shoulders. "That don't matter to me," he said, "but if you don't abandon this claim right now, I hereby summon you to appear before the gold commissioner one week from today. Meanwhile, you must cease and desist entering upon this land or working it." He handed a folded paper to Papa. The paper was sealed with a big red blob of wax. The man turned and marched away again.

Papa and I could not enjoy our luncheon. We puzzled over the paper. I can read a clear hand pretty well, but this writing was full of *whereas, henceforth, cease and desist*, and other long words, and neither Papa nor I could figure out what it was saying.

"It's lawyer papers," said Papa at last. "I never did like them, never could make much sense of them either. I wish Ma was here."

"Archie will know what to do," I said. "He can read this easily; so can Mrs. Mac. Archie will help us, Papa."

Our footsteps dragged as we walked back home. Archie had been home for dinner and had gone back to work. Mrs. Mac was lying down. Sometimes her leg still hurt where she had tripped over the dead creature our enemy Samuel Stokes had left on the front stoop not long before.

She heard us come in, though, and got up, drawing back the curtain that hid her and Archie's bed and chest of drawers. Mrs. Bowron had sent a message asking Mrs. Mac to put off the hospital ladies' meeting, so she was not going out after all. She shook her head at our news, and we puzzled over the summons together. "Let's set this aside until after supper," she said before long. "We'll make sense of it, Augustus, never fear.

Lisa, make a cup of tea for us, and let's have some music to raise our spirits."

Mrs. Mac sat down at her precious organ. Papa and I came and stood beside her. Today we sang some of the old hymns, "A Mighty Fortress Is Our God," "Rock of Ages," and my favourite, "Amazing Grace," and we were comforted, though still serious, when Archie finally came home. He made a long face at the summons, dashing our spirits more than a little.

"We'll take up this matter with the gold commissioner tomorrow," he said at last. "Let's hope he finds your ownership is good. However, if he orders you to do so, you must draw your stakes and abandon the claim. Perhaps you jumped too fast when you bought this property. You don't know much about mining or about the Cariboo."

Papa scowled. "Mostly I am a careful man," he said. "Maybe not careful enough this time. I have worked hard for my money; perhaps I have thrown it away."

"If you've been cheated, somebody has made a bad mistake, and that somebody is going to be sorry," I said furiously. I squeezed Papa's hand.

Archie nodded. "There's nothing to be done until we see the gold commissioner," he said. "That's our task for the morrow. Let's hope the rain holds off."

"Does this mean that Ma and the children may not be able to come to Cameronton?" I asked.

Papa looked at me unhappily. "We shall see," he said. "I have more bad news. I had hoped for good news to go with it, like finding gold on my new claim, but there's no use waiting now. Lisa, I sent for your trunk last winter. I knew you longed to have it."

"Papa, is the bad news about my trunk?"

His head drooped. "My friend wrote to tell me that his barn burned down. Nothing was saved. All the things that your ma and I had stored are gone, including your trunk. I am truly sorry, but that's what happened."

My eyes stung. Mama's pretty dresses—my real mother who died when I was born—all her pretty dresses, all the linens and blankets she had saved for when she had a home in her new country. All the china, shoes, and other things I couldn't even remember. Everything was gone.

Papa, as always, held out his arms, and I snuggled against his woolly waistcoat. After a while I felt his tears dampening my hair.

CHAPTER N.º 5

I thought I would be truly wretched the next morning when I woke up, but the day was bright and my spirits refused to remain low. It was my trunk that had burned, not my family. What mattered was getting all of us together again. What mattered was helping Papa.

Archie and Papa were almost ready to leave. Archie was dressed for business. He wore his black frock coat and high collar with his watch chain hanging across his waistcoat. His top hat sat squarely on his head. Papa had dressed in his Sunday best, his black suit and bowler hat. When

I came down in my good dress, Mrs. Mac's sprigged muslin that the dressmaker had made over for me, they both stared.

Mrs. Mac spoke up. "Lisa, surely you don't expect to go with the gentlemen!"

"I do," said I. "I must know what is happening. Don't you feel the same?"

Mrs. Mac laughed. "I must admit to some curiosity," she said, "and a very great interest, to be sure. However, this is not women's business."

"Papa, please?" I begged. "Archie?"

"In truth," said Papa, "I wish Ma was here. Don't think me ungrateful," he added, looking at Archie. "I am thankful for your friendship and support, but it would be a comfort if Lisa came as well."

With great relief I pulled my cloak around my shoulders and opened the door.

The September day was chilly, though the sun shone bright in the deep blue sky. The roads were still mired from melted snow, and I held my skirts up with both hands. Fortunately, I had not worn my Sunday shoes—my workday boots were soon muddy to the ankles.

We had to walk through Barkerville to Richfield, where the government buildings were located. "The way Barkerville is growing," said Archie, "it will soon take over Richfield, and Cameronton as well, I shouldn't wonder. Give it another year or two."

Papa seemed to rouse a little. However, his expression was blank; anybody could see he hadn't heard anything Archie had said. It was the first time in his life someone had accused him of dishonest dealing, and he was taking it badly. I myself felt almost as bad as if it had been my name on the summons instead of dear Papa's.

I had walked past the little group of buildings before but had never looked at them with the same interest as I did this morning, when so much depended on our success.

All of them gleamed with fresh white paint. A big Union Jack flew proudly from a tall flagstaff.

There was Judge Begbie's residence; next to it stood the gold commissioner's house, now occupied by Commissioner Ball and his family. The commissioner's office and the courtroom were two large rooms in the same building, built the year before, when Mr. Elwyn was the commissioner. The post office and the constables' office completed the little group.

We entered the office and walked toward the high counter. I hoped we would meet Commissioner Ball today. The miners respected him because he had taken troops to keep order in the Grouse Creek dispute. I didn't understand just what that was about, but Commissioner Ball had acted promptly to prevent a riot and nobody had been hurt.

"Not like in California," said James Wattie, who had learned the gold-mining business there. "Here in the Cariboo we have British law and order, under Britain's flag. I admire British law and order, and so would you, Lisa, if you ever found yourself deprived of it."

"Mr. McNaughton." A man perched on a copying stool wiped his nib on blotting paper and set his pen down carefully beside the biggest ledger I had ever seen. "What can I do for you this fine September day?"

"You can help my friend," said Archie confidently. "Mr. Schubert here has been summoned to appear on Monday. We need to talk to the commissioner and find out what's to be done."

"You've had your walk for nothing then," said the clerk. "Mr. Ball is out at the Prairie Flower mine today, checking a measurement." He smiled as he said Prairie Flower, and then his belly rumbled into laughter so strong that he doubled over as if in pain. At last he straightened up, with tears in his eyes.

Papa frowned. "I see nothing to laugh at," he said.

I spoke at the same time. "It's not funny," I said.

"Oh, oh," the clerk struggled. "Oh, I do apologize to all of you. Forgive me, it's nothing to do with you." He gulped and wheezed.

41

We stared at each other. "Are you in your right senses, sir?" Archie asked.

"Oh yes," said the clerk. "I was working at this very counter when the partners came in to register the name of their company. 'Cow Pat' Mine, can you believe it?"

He laughed again. "'I can't accept that registration,' I told them. I kept a straight face, but it wasn't easy.

"'What's wrong with it?' the fellow asked. 'It's pasture land, and cow pats is what it's full of. Haven't found anything better yet. We're hopeful there's gold, but right now there's cow pats.'

"'I better fetch the commissioner,' I said.

"Mr. Ball set them straight quick enough. 'Surely you want a sweeter-smelling name?' he said. 'One that a lady can mention without a blush.' They saw the point, thank goodness. That's when they came up with 'Prairie Flower.' I registered it fast enough, but it's hard not to laugh, remembering."

We were all smiling now. Mrs. Mac would not have blushed, I thought, but she would not use those words either. Ma would laugh almost as hard as the clerk, who now seemed eager to help. "May I see the summons?" he asked.

Papa handed it over. "Here's my bill of sale," he added. "I know the man who sold it to me. He came from Fort Garry, same as me."

"No cheats in Fort Garry?" asked the clerk dryly.

"I don't say that," Papa replied, "but Mr. Firman is not one of them."

"You'd best have him in court on Monday," said the clerk. "He'll be wanted."

Papa just stared. "Please sir," I spoke up. "I believe Mr. Firman has gone back to Fort Garry."

"Mr. Schubert?"

"My daughter is correct," Papa said slowly. "Mr. Firman acted on behalf of a dead man, and he has taken the money from the sale of the claim back to the widow."

"Ahhhh." The clerk drew out the exclamation. He looked sorry for Papa. "Well, Mr. Ball will get to the bottom of it. I will need a deposit of two pounds. This will be returned if the decision goes in your favour; if it goes against you, this money will be used to pay court costs. If I may say so, Mr. Schubert, you should be represented."

"And my bill of sale? Does that mean nothing? I paid for my claim."

"But," said the clerk, "did the seller have the right to sell it to you? That is yet to be determined. The plaintiff says they make all decisions concerning that property. You may know they hold five claims of two hundred feet each, and the two hundred feet in dispute is close to the shaft they have already sunk."

On that unhappy note, we left—after Papa had paid the two pounds. Our trip had not been wasted, but nothing had been settled, except that Papa would have to find money for a lawyer if he hoped to keep his claim.

CHAPTER N° 6

We walked in gloomy silence. Nobody could find a word to say. But then in my mind I climbed again over the pile of rock inside the adit; again, I caught the sheen of gold. Maybe one bad thing had happened. How bad? We would find out soon enough. But one very good thing had happened too.

With all the worry about Papa, I had hardly thought about my discovery. "We'll have to think of a wonderful name for our new mine," I said. "Let's all pick a name, then we can talk about it. And no cow pats. Who is at our tunnel today?"

Archie grinned. Even Papa worked up a little smile.

"Davie Ross and Adam Bailey have been guarding the entrance," Archie told me. "James and I have spelled them off as best we could. We have to keep active at our shaft site as well, or folks will ask what's wrong. Besides, the tighter we build our shelter, the easier it will be to work through the winter."

"I have not helped you so far." Papa shook his head. "I'll start tomorrow. There is little more I can do for myself except hire a lawyer."

"We may talk to the plaintiffs," said Archie. "I doubt a lawyer would help much. If James Wattie will speak for you, that would be best. He knows mining law as well as the commissioner. I've heard him in court. We'll be glad of your help on our claim, Augustus. We need every willing pair of hands."

"Mine too." I clenched my fists. "I can keep watch as well as anybody else—better, maybe. Nobody notices me when I ramble about. I can stay awake at night, too."

"No night watches, Lisa. Can you imagine what my wife would say?" Archie chuckled. "But you can certainly be part of the daytime detail."

CHAPTER N.º 7

Of course I could not spend all day at our diggings or at the tunnel. Mrs. Mac depended on me at home. One thing had changed. My copper and my washboard had been little used since Cariboo Cameron's big party in July. I did not do our washing any more, though I had done so much laundry on our journey overland to the Cariboo.

My hands had been red and cracked from lye soap and scrubbing. Now, while they were hard and calloused, they were no longer so ugly. I could swing a pickaxe without raising blisters.

I didn't want a lady's hands. My hands might not be soft like Mrs. Mac's, but she could never do a miner's work.

On Tuesday morning, my usual day, I set out to take our laundry to the Chinaman in Barkerville. The wash house was behind the Lung Duck Tong restaurant. My nose prickled as I smelled the food. I wished we would take our dinner there one day, but perhaps we would not be welcome, and perhaps the food did not taste as good as it smelled, though I wanted to try it for myself.

Behind the restaurant, the air was steamy. As soon as I entered the wash-house door, perspiration ran down my face and dampened my waist. No doubt the heat would be welcome in midwinter; now I wondered how any human beings could work in it, day in and day out. The owner had allowed me in the back room once, after I had begged to see his boilers. Three huge fires burned under three giant coppers; three witch-figures stirred the boiling clothes with wooden paddles, all misty in the steam. I used to be proud of my wash, but I never got my sheets and shirts as white as Ah Lee and his workers did.

I carried the week's wash in a big bag over my shoulder, as usual, and paused to sniff the clean clothes I picked up in exchange, fragrant with drying in the wind and sun. I was in so much of a hurry to get to our mine that my other errand went clean out of my head and I might never have thought of it until I reached home if I hadn't been interrupted.

"Good day, Miss Lucky Lisa," boomed a voice.

"Good day to you also, Mr. Moses." I smiled up at the portly black man in the starched white jacket—and remembered. "My errand is to your shop, and I would have walked right by if you had not spoken. Ma would say my wits were wool-gathering!"

"You'd'a seen my pole, surely." The man gestured to the fat barbershop pole by his front door. Red and white stripes twisted their way from top to bottom. "My goodness, Miss Lisa, it's the biggest barbershop pole in the Cariboo. How

I carried the week's wash in a big bag over my shoulder, as usual, and paused to sniff the clean clothes I picked up in exchange, fragrant with drying in the wind and sun.

many times have I told you?" He chuckled. "That there pole is hard to miss. So, what can I do for you, pretty lady? Not chop off your golden curls, that I would *not* do, even if you asked."

Mr. Moses held the door open and bowed me into his little shop.

He lifted the flap and took his place behind the polished mahogany counter. Behind him, the upper shelves were lined with his customers' shaving mugs. Archie's name, "A. McNaughton," was written on his mug in black paint edged with gold. Beside the name, the artist had painted a lady in a purple dress sitting on a pink and gold couch. When Mr. Moses gave Archie a shave, he whipped up a lather in that mug and painted Archie's whiskers with the white cream.

Bottles of Wellington Delaney Moses' Hair Invigorator packed the middle shelf. Although I could not read the small print, I knew the label promised to "restore hair that has fallen off or become thin . . . relieve the Headache, and give the hair a darker and glossy colour."

"One bottle, please." I pointed, and Mr. Moses took it down, tore a piece of brown paper off the roll, and wrapped the bottle deftly, almost in a single motion, handing it to me with a bow. "On Mr. Wattie's account, please," I said.

Mr. Moses was famous in the Cariboo because he had helped to catch a murderer. If I had not been in a hurry, I would have stayed to talk to him. I smiled again and waved as I left. Mr. Moses waved back.

Mrs. Mac had dinner on the table when I got home, but only the two of us sat down to eat. Archie and Papa were too busy to come home.

"Off you go, Lisa," said Mrs. Mac, when I set down my knife and fork. "I'll put away the laundry."

The rest of that day—and the rest of that week—passed. Sometimes the hours raced; sometimes they crawled. I kept watch on the adit and searched for more gold nuggets and carried food and water to the others. The housing above our shaft grew slowly. The work would have gone faster with nails, but nails were as scarce as gold in the Cariboo and almost as valuable. For hours on end I handed up wooden dowels and held the auger while the dowels were fitted into place and another squared log was hoisted up, then I handed up the auger so Papa could drill more holes.

The two plaintiffs named in the summons had taken Barnard's Express down to Yale, so Papa and Archie could not speak to them, though they were expected back for court. Rumour had it they had taken their gold dust to the bank.

Some folks don't want to trust their gold to anybody, though Barnard's Express has never been robbed. Gold shipments were carried in a safe. Robbers held up the stage one time and got the safe, but they couldn't open it and couldn't carry off the heavy thing by horseback. They finally had to leave it, and the driver came back with his wagon and picked it up.

CHAPTER N.º 8

James Wattie had agreed to speak for Papa in court. "I'm mighty thankful for your help with our building," he told Papa. "You are more of a carpenter than the rest of us put together."

Papa was pleased. "I'm beholden to you and Archie for your help in my affairs," he had replied.

Mr. Wattie knocked early on Monday morning. The wind blew him in through the door. All the other grown-ups had told me I could not go, but I still hoped Mr. Wattie would say I could. That hope, however, was in vain. "Court is no place for a bairn," he decreed. "You'd best stay home with Mrs. McNaughton."

"I'm restless too, Lisa," said Mrs. Mac. "Suppose we both go out to our claims. You can show me what you've found in the tunnel."

"Elizabeth, you cannot possibly climb rock piles in hoop skirts and petticoats." We all stared at Archie. I had never heard him speak sharply to his wife. Nor, I think, had she. Her face flamed.

Mr. Wattie stepped in before she could reply. "I have a better idea," he said briskly. "Our new hospital is not officially open, but we have patients already. Could the two of you help Dr. Black today?"

A long look passed between Archie and his wife. He made a gesture of apology but did not speak.

"I'll go, and gladly," I said.

"We'll both go," said Mrs. Mac.

We hurried through the rain, which now poured down. One horse-drawn cart jolted past us, then a second, with a canvas top. Maybe we would drive a cart like that when we were rich.

Dr. Black greeted us. "A hospital is not a place for too much modesty," he said brusquely. "Do what you can. If you feel faint, sit down and take a drink of water."

Mrs. Mac took out her vial of smelling salts, and the surgeon nodded. "We have two broken legs," he said, "and another leg, crushed by a cave-in, which I must amputate this afternoon. Dr. Russell will assist; two men will hold the patient while we operate. Don't think of staying for the surgery, ladies—you won't enjoy it. But your help this morning is very welcome, and there's plenty to do. Please start by washing these three patients, as best you can. Don't disturb the bandages."

He continued, "Two men have fevers. Use cloths dipped in cold water to cool them. The only other patient"—he pointed toward a makeshift screen— "has a nurse." He bustled off to the surgery.

Mrs. Mac lifted a leather bucket and poured water into a basin. I found a bundle of cloths and gave them to her.

Why was one patient hidden? I peeked behind the screen. A figure in a white nightgown—a woman, surely—heaved herself to and fro, muttering. Long hair hid her face. There was no nurse in sight. I ran to the bed.

"I'm here," I said. "Let me help you."

A bony hand gripped my arm. Then I saw the bands of linen and understood why she was struggling. This woman had been tied to the bed. Gently I put back her hair. Her face was burning hot; her dark eyes glittered. She breathed with difficulty, and her breath rattled. I had never seen her except in her hurdy-gurdy costume with the huge dark blue hoop skirt and the red-patterned shirt-waist and her hair in a top-knot. I had thought Fraulein Greta was a big woman. Now I saw how thin she was, how small.

"Help," she muttered, and again, "Help." Even her voice was small, as if she was sure no help would come. "Must go. Court today, must go." Her eyes moved past me; she gave no sign that we had ever met.

I had not moved from her bedside when Fraulein Lili arrived. I still felt numb. We greeted each other as if this was nothing out of the ordinary, as if we met often beside a hospital bed.

"Is she still trying to get up?" Lili asked.

"She wants to go to court," I explained. "Why I don't know, but she must not go out into the cold rain. I'll get some water and a cloth." I stood up.

"Sit down, Lisa," said Lili. "I'll bring them." She came back quickly. I bathed Greta's face while Lili unbuttoned the high-necked nightshirt and put cool cloths against her friend's bony chest.

"She has been dancing every night," said Lili, "all night, as long as she had partners. Going to court costs money. I wish Samuel Stokes had died at birth." She spat out the words. "The first night of the snowstorm, nobody wanted to go home. Greta danced until morning, then she went out into the snow in her light shoes and a summer coat. She took cold; the cold turned feverish; now the doctor says she has pneumonia. If she keeps wasting her strength trying to get up, she'll die. She may die anyway."

"What is her case?" I asked. "Papa is in court today. He may know what happened. If not, he can find out." Why should I have thought Papa's case would be the only one today?

"I forget," said Lili. "She has three of them, about loans that Samuel Stokes got because he was going to marry her. He bought an interest in two mining companies, and this is one of them, but I can't remember the name."

Greta began talking again, a long stream of something, interrupted by the rattling breaths. I heard the odd word, but there was no sense to it. The breathing became noisier, a fit of wheezing and coughing. Mrs. Mac appeared, then Dr. Black.

"Out, all of you," he commanded. He stopped Lili. "You stay," he said. "Hold her down if she tries to get up. I'll give her a dose of laudanum, enough to make her sleepy. Can you stay all night?"

I heard Lili say she could stay. Dr. Black emerged, on his way to fetch the laudanum. "Thank you for this morning," he said to Mrs. Mac and me, nodding toward the door. "Can you come again, say, on Wednesday morning?"

"We'll be here," said Mrs. Mac.

"It's odd that Papa and Fraulein Greta had cases in court on the same day, don't you think?" I said, as we walked homeward in the rain.

"Maybe," said Mrs. Mac. "I don't know anything about court cases."

"I want to learn," I said. "Papa is afraid of lawyer papers. I don't want to be afraid like him."

"You'll need to go to school," said Mrs. Mac.

"I went to school in Fort Garry," I said. "I learned to read and write. I learned my times tables up to twelve."

"That's enough for some people," said Mrs. Mac, "but not for you, if you want to understand lawyer papers."

"There is no school here," I said slowly.

"Not yet," Mrs. Mac agreed. "Somebody could start a school for miners this winter. Many of them cannot read or write; they can be cheated so easily. One or two evenings a week would be enough to begin, to see how it went. My father employed an English governess for me, Miss Arabella Smithers. Miss Smithers was a bluestocking. She loved learning, and thought every girl should be like her."

"Are you a bluestocking, Mrs. McNaughton?" I did not know what she meant.

"I like to explore new ideas. I like to read," said Mrs. Mac, "and I believe in education for girls— they should at least learn to read and write. However, I would not give up the chance to marry and make a home in order to study and to teach others, like Miss Smithers. You could learn everything from her, Lisa. If you wanted to study something she did not already know, she would find a way to learn about it and help you do the same. She teaches now at Mrs. Simpson's Ladies School on Mansfield Street in Montreal."

"Montreal!" I was horrified. "That's even farther than Fort Garry, and it took us five months to get from there to Kamloops!"

Mrs. Mac sighed. "I'd ask you to think on it, Lisa. We'll talk another time. I do hope court has gone well for your papa today."

The rain still drove down. When we reached home, we hurried to put on dry clothes and get warm. I had left a big pot of soup on the stove. We both ate a small bowl of it.

Before long, the men arrived, stamping their feet and shaking their soggy coats. Papa's shoulders slumped. Rain ran in rivulets from the rim of his bowler. "That's the end of me," said Papa. "That Last Chance Company holds the right to mine my claim; if they find gold, it belongs to them. I own the land, but not the minerals underneath it. Tomorrow I must pull up my stakes."

CHAPTER N° 9

"*Papa, that's dreadful. The judge must be* wrong. What can you do?"

"Nothing," said Papa. "Six months ago I could have appealed this ruling to Governor Douglas in Victoria, but then a lot of miners signed a petition asking the governor to forbid appeals against a gold commissioner's ruling."

"That was when we had a first-rate gold commissioner," said Archie. "Plenty of men who signed that petition wish they hadn't now, but the governor won't change the law back again."

"For now, Ma and the children can't come to the Cariboo," said Papa. "Maybe I'll go prospecting. I have to make money somehow."

"You'd be a fool to go prospecting now," Archie told him. "Winter is in the air."

"I already found gold," I said.

"We may have a mine," said Archie, "and we may not. We won't know before spring, and maybe not before summer."

"Papa, Fraulein Greta is sick in the hospital," I said. "Did you hear anything about her court case?"

"The only case in court today was mine," said Papa bitterly, "and I heard more than enough about that one. Court was adjourned as soon as the commissioner made his ruling."

"Strange," said Mrs. Mac. "Greta was trying to get out of bed to go to court. She was sure her case would be heard today."

"Papa, will you come with me to the hospital tomorrow?" I asked. "I was not in court. Why should Greta believe what I say? You were there, and you can explain everything to her in her own language. Maybe you can find out why she is so troubled."

"Perhaps you should both wait until Wednesday," said Mrs. Mac. "Fraulein Greta is very ill. You may not be able to talk to her at all."

"She won't rest until she knows about her case," I said. "Please, Papa."

"*Ja*," said Papa. That was one German word I knew: yes. "You want to know how she is, Lisa. We will go in the morning, even if the poor woman is too ill to see us. I will help if I can."

Fraulein Greta wheezed and gasped. "You may stay for five minutes," Dr. Black told us. "No more. Don't be surprised if she mistakes you for somebody else."

Lili sat beside her friend. "You look as if you didn't sleep all night," I said to her. Lili nodded.

"There's an empty bed in the corner," I told her. "Lie down and close your eyes while we are here."

Fraulein Greta recognized me at once. When Papa talked to her in German, her face lit up. She gripped his hand and held it with both of hers. Anybody would have thought they had been friends all their lives. Soon, however, Greta stopped smiling. She kept shaking her head then began to struggle again, trying to get out of bed. Papa looked at me. "She is talking about the Last Chance Mining Company," he said slowly.

Greta threw up her hands. Tears poured out of her eyes. Dr. Black pulled back the makeshift curtain. "Out, both of you," he ordered. "Now."

We scrambled toward the door. Lili, snoring lightly, did not stir as we tiptoed past her bed.

"Fraulein Greta's case is the same as yours but she's on the other side," I said. "How can this be? She has never seen you before today. Why should she sue you, Papa?"

"I don't know," said Papa. "She is not the only one, though. Two men from the Last Chance

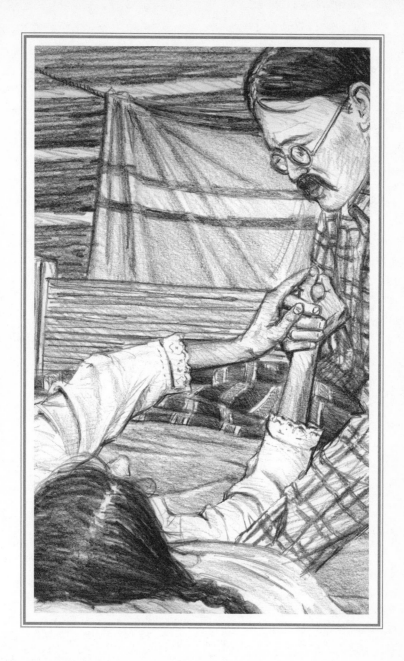

When Papa talked to Greta in German, her face lit up. She gripped his hand and held it with both of hers. Anybody would have thought they had been friends all their lives.

Company came to court yesterday. They brought the agreement that made Commissioner Bell rule against me."

Dinner that day was gloomy. Papa went off to our diggings as soon as he had finished. I kneaded fresh bread and set it to rise, but a draft must have got at it, or maybe my sourdough was old—the loaves were small. The fresh bread smell, when I finally baked the loaves, did not raise my spirits.

It was almost dark when somebody knocked. I opened the door and saw the familiar blue skirt and patterned red blouse that the hurdy-gurdies wore. The woman who entered was young, and I had never seen her before; she must have been a new arrival. As soon as she spoke, I was sure she was. "You, Lisa?" Her voice was hesitant, her accent heavy.

"Yes, I am Lisa."

She held out a folded piece of paper. As I took it, she turned to go. "Wait," I said. "What is this? Who sent you?"

"For you," she said. "Lili." Then she was gone, the door thudding closed behind her.

I sat down and turned up the lamp.

"Der Lisa," the letter began.

I rite fur Greta. She wuri wuri all day. Doan wanna hert yur fader, no nevr. Doan wanna hert yu. She wanna be partners. Yu cum sune nuther day, yu an fader, sine paper. This Greta want. Yrs rizpekfuly, Lili.

I never read worse spelling, or a more welcome message. Greta wanted Papa and me to be her partners, it seemed. When Papa and Archie came home, I read the letter to both of them. Then everybody took a turn reading it.

"It's clear enough, if she means it," said Archie.

"I'm sure she means it," I said.

"I think so too," Mrs. Mac agreed.

"That's the best news I could have," said Papa. "Please gather round, all of you. Let us all thank our God for this." He knelt on the dirt floor; so did Archie, Mrs. Mac, and I. All of us bowed our heads.

I slept well and woke early. So, it seemed, did the others. Papa poured me a cup of coffee. Mrs. Mac had put some of our precious butter on the toast and opened her only jar of gooseberry preserves. I love the tart berries, and these were the first I had tasted since Fort Garry, years ago. Nobody took more than a spoonful, but I heaped mine. We all spread it on our toast and ate it in little bites to make it last.

"That is a breakfast to remember." Archie spoke for all of us. He bent over his wife and brushed her cheek lovingly. "I'll not be home for dinner, my dear. Lisa, Augustus, I am thankful for you both, and will be more so when papers are signed."

We were out the door soon after him, walking briskly through the frosty morning. Inside the hospital, my eyes went at once to the corner, to the screen that hid Fraulein Greta's bed.

But there was no screen. No screen, only the rough bedstead with a straw mattress on top of the boards.

"Dr. Black!" I cried. The man whose leg had been amputated opened pain-filled eyes; other patients stirred.

Dr. Black opened his surgery door. His clothes were rumpled, his hair unbrushed. "Ah," he said. "You knew her, didn't you."

"She is dead, then," said Papa dully.

"Early this morning," said Dr. Black. "We did our best, but she was too weak. Her friend arranged for men to take her body. I'm sorry, but I don't know where she would be laid out. They'll know at the hotel. Perhaps you ladies will not want to stay this morning. I can send for other helpers, if you wish."

"I will stay," said Mrs. Mac at once. "Lisa, why

don't you go with your papa to find Fraulein
Lili."

Papa, who had been so cheerful, looked as if he
had been whipped. "Papa," I began. My voice
choked, but then I got it back. "Papa, I will stay
with Mrs. Mac. It is my duty." I ran to him. "Papa,
I am sorry, so sorry." We hugged each other.

"I too am sorry," Papa said. "Sorry for Miss Greta
and Miss Lili, and sorry for myself and you as
well, and for Ma and the children who did not
know to be glad and then sad again." He shook
his head. "We are alive and well," he said. "I will
work with Archie and James and the others this
morning after all."

"Duty." Mrs. Mac gave a funny little laugh.
"I have taught you something after all, Lisa. Good
for you, my girl."

Perhaps Mrs. Mac had never completely
approved of anything I did before, but her
approval now was the sweeter for that, and we
worked together with a will that morning. After
the patients had had their breakfast of porridge

and cream from the Wake Up, Jake Restaurant, we washed them and changed bed linens. I read a story by Mr. Edgar Allan Poe to the man who had lost his leg. It was a scary story, but he listened to every word, and for that time, at least, I believe he forgot his pain.

At noon, we went on our way.

"We won't go home for dinner, Lisa," said Mrs. Mac. "If you agree, we'll look for Fraulein Lili now."

I agreed right away. The clerk at the Occidental Hotel sent us to a little chapel behind the saloon where Fraulein Greta had danced. There we found Lili and other hurdy-gurdy dancers. A priest knelt beside a trestle table, where Greta's body lay. She was dressed in her favourite dress, of rose-coloured silk. She had worn that dress to church when the banns of marriage were read for her and Samuel Stokes, although they had not married, thanks to me. Her hair was brushed and curled in ringlets around her face. "She is beautiful," I whispered.

Lili, sitting beside her friend, looked up. "Beautiful," she echoed.

"This is a sad day for you," said Mrs. Mac to Lili.

"Yes," Lili replied. "But one thing is easy now. I stayed here to help my friend. Almost I am caught by winter. But not quite. I leave for California next week. Or Victoria, maybe. I will miss you, Lisa."

"Will you write?" I asked.

She laughed. "You got my note?" she replied. "I don't write so good, do I!"

"We slept well last night because of your letter," said Mrs. Mac, "even though the news was twice as bad this morning."

"Papers," said Lili.

"Greta will never sign them now." Mrs. Mac said what I was thinking. "I am sorry for her death, of course, and so is Lisa, who knew her better than I did. But we are also sad for Augustus Schubert, who would so gladly have been Greta's partner if she had lived."

"Partner," said Lili. "My goodness, you don't know! Greta signed the papers yesterday afternoon. Her lawyer brought them, and Greta signed. Dr. Black signed. Man without leg signed. Go see that lawyer, he will explain. Don't worry, Greta signed them."

She told us the lawyer's name and address. "Go and see him now," she said.

"Tomorrow is time enough," said Mrs. Mac. "We came to be with you, Fraulein Lili—unless you wish us to come at another time."

"No, no, stay," said Lili at once.

"You are really going away next week?" I asked. "Won't you ever come back?"

"No," said Lili. "Like I told you, I'll look for a husband—a farmer, not a mining man. Raise chickens, ducks, maybe a family." She smiled.

We visited with Lili for most of the afternoon. "If you stay in Victoria, you may see Lisa there one day," said Mrs. Mac, as we began to get ready to leave at last. I looked at her in astonishment.

"At school, perhaps," Mrs. Mac continued, "or on her way to school somewhere. Who knows?"

"School." Lili rolled the word around on her tongue. "School is good. Lisa, go to school. I wish I had."

"But I love the Cariboo," I said. "You know I want to be a miner."

"Be a miner who went to school, then," said Lili. "If I stay in Victoria, I'll leave a message for you at the Registry Office there."

CHAPTER N⁰ 10

Once again we passed a hopeful night, though nobody slept as well as the night before. On Thursday morning Papa and I set out to see the lawyer. Mrs. Mac and Archie did not come. "Whatever this is, it concerns you two, not us," Archie said. "We will hope you bring back good news."

The lawyer was old. His hair and whiskers were white; his face was a hillside of ridges and valleys. "Come in," he said. "Fraulein Lili told me to expect you." His smile showed gaps where teeth were missing. "You are here about

Fraulein Greta's will," he said.

"We were told that Fraulein Greta signed papers, nothing more," said Papa.

"Ah," said the lawyer. "It's all proper, I can tell you, signed and witnessed. Just between us, it's as well that Fraulein Lili is the only beneficiary— besides yourself, young lady." The gap-toothed smile was aimed in my direction.

"I don't understand," I said, wishing Archie or Mrs. Mac were there.

"I will explain," said the lawyer. "Fraulein Greta was out of her mind with fever, though not when she told me what she wanted, and not when she signed her will. That's my legal opinion. However, another lawyer might form a different opinion. Miss Lisa, you benefit by this will, and so does Fraulein Lili. Fraulein Lili is happy for you, and happy that her friend did what she wanted; she will not argue. Is that clear?"

"Yes, sir," I said.

"Good. I will continue. By her new will, Fraulein Greta leaves her interest in the Last

Chance Mining Company to Miss Lisa Schubert. That is you, young lady, is it not?"

"Yes, sir," I said again.

"It is not written in the will," said the lawyer, "but my client told me that Mr. Augustus Schubert would likely look after this property for Miss Schubert. That is you, sir, I believe." The smile was turned on Papa.

"Yes, sir," Papa said, borrowing my words.

"Yes," said the lawyer. "The balance of Fraulein Greta's estate is left to her friend Fraulein Lili. We are converting these assets to cash, as Miss Lili intends to leave the Cariboo. What are your intentions, Miss Schubert? Will you keep your inheritance, or will you sell it? There is no rush to decide—take your time. You are very young; get advice from your elders. From me, if you wish."

"I don't need time," I said. "Fraulein Greta has been very good to us. I will keep what she has left to me. Papa, will you help me?"

"Of course," said Papa. "We can talk things over with Archie and James Wattie as well."

The lawyer was old ... His smile showed gaps where teeth were missing. "You are here about Fraulein Greta's will,"
he said.

"James Wattie, now there's a wise man," said the lawyer, "and a man who knows all about the mining business. You can depend on him."

We all went to Fraulein Greta's funeral the next day—Papa and I, Mrs. Mac and Archie. Mr. Wattie joined us. "Most ladies won't come to bury a dance-hall girl," he told Mrs. Mac and me. "I'm glad you are here, Mrs. McNaughton, Lisa."

"She was my friend," I said. "Papa and I will always be grateful to her."

"I too will remember her in my prayers," said Mrs. Mac.

At the cemetery, a deep grave had been dug. "If she had died a month later," said Archie, "the ground would have been frozen too deep to dig.

The body would have had to wait until spring."
I shuddered.

Reverend Evans led us in prayers for the dead.
I noticed a priest among the mourners and
was surprised to recognize Father Grandidier.
I remembered him on the way to the Cariboo.
A miner had tried to kick him into the fire when
he knelt to pray.

Archie and Mrs. Mac remembered him too, and
soon he was meeting Papa and talking to all of us.
Greta had not been Catholic, but some other
hurdy-gurdies were, and he had known Fraulein
Greta and liked her. "Lisa, you are growing up," he
said. "What are your plans?"

"I intend to go to school," I said, "to learn what
I need to know about being a miner and, I hope,
a mine owner some day."

Father Grandidier looked at me sharply.

"Lisa could study in Montreal," said Mrs. Mac.
"I hope she decides to do that."

Archie smiled. "My wife told me about
Mrs. Simpson's new school," he said. "Montreal is

an exciting city, Lisa. We both have family there. You would be well looked after."

Papa frowned. "Montreal is too far away," he said.

"I agree," I said.

"God moves in mysterious ways," said Father Grandidier. "The Sisters of St. Ann run the best school in the country, in Victoria."

"I've heard that the governor's daughters were expelled from that school because they attended a government ball," said Mrs. Mac. "Lisa won't learn to be a lady there."

"The rules are strict," Father Grandidier admitted. "Pupils at St. Ann's are not allowed to attend a dance, let alone waltz with young men, as the governor's daughters did." He shook his head. "Governor Douglas thought the Sisters would change the rules for his daughters because they were his hostesses, but of course the nuns would not do that. The Sisters are very thorough in all they do. They are starting a school in New Westminster a year from now. If you go there, Lisa, you will get a good education. You will also be able to return to the Cariboo from May to September, when the school is closed."

"I can be a miner all summer!" I beamed. It seemed too good to be true.

"Exactly," he said. "In three or four years, the Sisters will teach you everything."

Papa looked at Father Grandidier, then at Mrs. Mac. "I like this idea better than Montreal," he said.

"You are not Catholic, are you?" asked Mrs. Mac.

"No," Papa replied. "My family has been Lutheran for nearly four hundred years. I expect one of my ancestors stood beside Martin Luther when he nailed his famous theses to the cathedral door. My dear wife is Catholic born and bred, though. Lisa, Ma would be very happy if you study at a convent school."

"That's settled then," I said. "Archie, Mrs. Mac, I'll stay here if you'll have me until Ma is here. I'll work and learn here until the new school opens, and I will come back every summer."

"You have brought us luck all along," Mr. Wattie said.

"If you want to manage a mine, I believe you will," said Archie. "People will tell you no woman can do that. Don't believe them. A few women have always managed things, although the world has not always known what they did."

"You know more about mining than I do," said Papa.

"Archie," said Mr. Wattie, "do you have any strong drink in the house? I would propose a toast."

"We have no strong drink," said Mrs. Mac. "Would you drink your toast in water? Mr. McNaughton, please bring the crystal goblets."

Archie climbed on a chair. One by one, he handed down five long-stemmed glasses, cut in a pattern of Scotch thistles, from the highest cupboard. They reflected the lamp light, glinting like diamonds. Mrs. Mac half-filled each one with water. I sat while the others stood. Mr. Wattie raised his glass.

"To Lisa," he said. "May her future be bright. May her golden dreams come true."

Archie and Mrs. Mac and dear Papa raised their glasses, smiling at me. "A bright future and golden dreams, Lisa," they said.

Acknowledgements

Many of the same sources that so richly contributed to previous volumes in this series continued to help in my research for Book 4, including the Internet, my own library, and the Robarts Library at the University of Toronto. Family records, including photographs and letters as well as a few treasured articles from the period, helped me with authentic details of fashion, language, and home life in Lisa's time.

Material about the Schubert family previously supplied by Elizabeth Duckworth of the Kamloops Museum and by Mickey King, archivist with the Sisters of St. Ann, has provided valuable data for this volume.

My writing group has been generous with support and criticism for more than twenty-five years; thanks yet again, Ayanna, Barb, Heather, Lorraine, Pat, Sylvia, and Vancy.

Dear Reader,

This has been the fourth and final book about Lisa. We hope you've enjoyed meeting and getting to know her as much as we have enjoyed bringing her—and her wonderful story—to you.

Although Lisa's tale is told, there are still eleven more terrific girls to read about, whose exciting adventures take place in Canada's past—girls just like you. So do keep on reading!

And please—don't forget to keep in touch! We love receiving your incredible letters telling us about your favourite stories and which girls you like best. And thank you for telling us about the stories you would like to read! There are so many remarkable stories in Canadian history. It seems that wherever we live, great stories live too, in our towns and cities, on our rivers and mountains. We hope that Our Canadian Girl *captures the richness of that past.*

Sincerely,
Barbara Berson
Editor

Canada's

1608
Samuel de Champlain establishes the first fortified trading post at Quebec.

1759
The British defeat the French in the Battle of the Plains of Abraham.

1812
The United States declares war against Canada.

1845
The expedition of Sir John Franklin to the Arctic ends when the ship is frozen in the pack ice; the fate of its crew remains a mystery.

1869
Louis Riel leads his Métis followers in the Red River Rebellion.

1871
British Columbia joins Canada.

1755
The British expel the entire French population of Acadia (today's Maritime provinces), sending them into exile.

1776
The 13 Colonies revolt against Britain, and the Loyalists flee to Canada.

1762
Elizabeth

1837
Calling for responsible government, the Patriotes, following Louis-Joseph Papineau, rebel in Lower Canada; William Lyon Mackenzie leads the uprising in Upper Canada.

1863
Lisa

1867
New Brunswick, Nova Scotia, and the United Province of Canada come together in Confederation to form the Dominion of Canada.

1870
Manitoba joins Canada. The Northwest Territories become an official territory of Canada.